Lola Loves
Stories

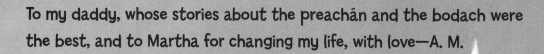

To my daddy, whose stories about the preachán and the bodach were the best, and to Martha for changing my life, with love—A. M.

To Marion and the magnificent Milroys, with love—R. B.

ISBN 978-0-545-29694-6

Text copyright © 2010 by Anna McQuinn. Illustrations copyright © 2009, 2010 by Rosalind Beardshaw. All rights reserved. Published by Scholastic Inc., 557 Broadway, New York, NY 10012, by arrangement with Charlesbridge Publishing, Inc. SCHOLASTIC and associated logos are trademarks and/or registered trademarks of Scholastic Inc.

25   22/0

Printed in the U.S.A.   40

First Scholastic printing, October 2010

Illustrations done in acrylic on paper
Display type and text type set in Garamouche Bold and Billy
Designed by Martha MacLeod Sikkema

First published in the United Kingdom in 2009 by Alanna Books,
46 Chalvey Road East, Slough, Berkshire, SL1 2LR, United Kingdom,
as *Lulu Loves Stories*. Copyright © 2009 by Alanna Books.

Lola Loves Stories

Anna McQuinn
Illustrated by Rosalind Beardshaw

SCHOLASTIC INC.
New York Toronto London Auckland
Sydney Mexico City New Delhi Hong Kong

Lola's daddy takes her to the library on Saturdays.

The library is *very* busy,

but Lola finds some excellent books.

Lola's daddy reads the
first story at home.
It is about a
fairy princess.

All the next day
Lola wears a fancy dress
and a sparkly crown.
She is a fabulous fairy princess!

On Sunday night Lola and her mommy read the next story. It is about an amazing journey.

On Monday Lola takes her friends on fantastic trips to places like Paris and Lagos.

On Tuesday Lola chooses a story
about friends.

All afternoon she and Ben play with their babies. Lola has cappuccino, and her baby has juice.

Tuesday night Lola's mommy reads
a story about fierce tigers.

The next day Lola chases her friend
Orla all over the jungle.

On Wednesday night Lola reads
a story about Old MacDonald.
The next day she is a farmer.
Lola's cow has a boo-boo!

Mommy knows how to fix it.

On Thursday night Lola and her daddy read about building.

The next day Lola fixes up her house.
She needs a hammer, a saw . . .
and a little help from her daddy.

On Friday night Lola's daddy
makes up a story about
magic shoes. The next day
Lola's shoes are truly amazing.

They sparkle all the way
to the library . . .

. . . and all the way home.

They even sparkle while her daddy reads her a story about a wild and wicked monster!

What will Lola be tomorrow?